The Lucky Horseshoes

The
Lucky Horseshoes

At the end of the riding lesson, Red and Sue helped all the riders dismount.

"Now we're going to have a parade," Red announced. "Each one of you can lead your pony back into the stable."

Nancy led Cupid into his stall. Then she went into the tack room with Bess and George.

" 'Bye, Nancy," Jackie said as she headed toward the exit.

" 'Bye!" Nancy called.

Katie walked past, too. But she didn't say goodbye to Bess or Nancy or George. Nancy thought Katie was acting silly.

"Oh, no!" Bess yelled. She was staring into her lunch box.

"What's wrong?" Nancy asked.

"My lucky earrings are gone!" Bess cried.

The Nancy Drew Notebooks

THE
NANCY DREW
NOTEBOOKS®

#26

The Lucky Horseshoes

CAROLYN KEENE
ILLUSTRATED BY ANTHONY ACCARDO

Aladdin Paperbacks
New York London Toronto Sydney Singapore

First Aladdin Paperbacks edition February 2003
First Minstrel Books edition September 1998

Copyright © 1998 by Simon & Schuster, Inc.
Produced by Mega-Books, Inc.

ALADDIN PAPERBACKS
An imprint of Simon & Schuster
Children's Publishing Division
1230 Avenue of the Americas
New York, NY 10020

The text of this book was set in Excelsior.

Printed in the United States of America
10 9 8 7 6

NANCY DREW and THE NANCY DREW NOTEBOOKS
are registered trademarks of Simon & Schuster, Inc.

ISBN 0-671-00822-6

1

Squishy Mud

One minute of school left," eight-year-old Nancy Drew whispered. It was Thursday afternoon.

"That's only sixty seconds," Bess Marvin whispered back. Bess was one of Nancy's two best friends. Her blue eyes were bright with excitement.

George Fayne was Nancy's other best friend. George sat at the front of the row. Nancy could tell George was excited, too. Her shiny dark curls bounced as she moved around in her seat.

"Fifty-five seconds," Nancy whispered. "Fifty-four, fifty-three . . ."

Nancy tried to sit still, but she was

too excited. She and Bess and George were taking their first riding lesson after school.

"May I have your attention, please?" Mrs. Reynolds asked. She was the girls' third-grade teacher at Carl Sandburg Elementary School.

"Tomorrow morning is our classroom spelling bee," Mrs. Reynolds said. "I want everyone to get plenty of sleep tonight—"

Brring! The final bell rang.

"And come to school tomorrow with your spelling caps on," Mrs. Reynolds finished. "Class dismissed!"

Nancy, Bess, and George jumped up from their seats. They put on their jackets and gathered their things. Then they hurried out of the classroom. They walked as quickly as they could down the hallway.

"See you at the stables!" Katie Zaleski called as they opened the front door to the school and stepped outside. She was starting riding lessons that afternoon, too.

Katie hurried toward her mother's car. Nancy, Bess, and George sat on the front steps of the school.

"I hope Hannah comes soon," Nancy said. "I don't want us to be late getting to the stable."

Hannah Gruen was the Drew family's housekeeper. She had lived with Nancy and her father ever since Nancy's mother had died, five years earlier.

The girls piled into the car as soon as Hannah pulled up. As Hannah drove, the girls chattered about their new after-school activity.

"What did you girls have for lunch today?" Hannah asked.

"*Jumping* beans," George said with a giggle.

Hannah looked at them through the rearview mirror. Nancy could see that Hannah was smiling.

Nancy, Bess, and George settled down and looked out the window for the turnoff.

Soon the car reached the part of town where the houses were spread far apart. Hannah slowed the car. Then she turned into a drive marked with a sign that said River Heights Riding Academy. She parked in front of the stable.

Inside, ponies and horses stood in stalls. Nancy heard them snorting and stomping.

A tall, red-haired man came out of the office. He was followed by a woman with blond hair. "May I help you folks?" the man asked.

"We're here for our first riding lesson," Nancy told him.

"Great!" the man said. "My name is Red. I'll be your instructor." He turned to the blond woman. "And this is Sue, my assistant. She'll show you around the stable."

"You can keep your school things in the tack room," Sue told the girls. "I'll show you where it is."

Nancy and her friends followed Sue into the stable and into a tiny room. The room was filled with brooms, buckets, brushes, and saddles. The floor was muddy. Cubbies lined one wall.

Bess and George put their jackets and knapsacks away. Nancy didn't have to. Her things were still in Hannah's car.

The girls hurried to the riding ring. A few boys and girls were already waiting to begin their lesson.

Katie was standing with Mandy Trout. Mandy was a girl Nancy knew from ice-skating. Katie and Mandy were talking to Jackie Taylor. Jackie lived near George. They sometimes played basketball together in George's driveway.

George, Bess, and Nancy walked over to join the other girls.

"Are you excited about your first riding lesson?" Bess asked Mandy.

"This isn't my first lesson," Mandy said. "I've been riding for two months already."

"It's my first," Jackie said.

"I knew that the minute you walked in," Mandy told Jackie.

Mandy pointed to Jackie's white pants. "Nobody wears white pants for riding," she said. "Those are going to get good and dirty."

Jackie looked down at her pants. Her face turned pink. Nancy knew Jackie felt embarrassed.

"I didn't know what to wear, either," Nancy said. She wanted to make Jackie feel better.

"All you have to do is look at me," Mandy announced. She spun around so that everyone could see what she was wearing. "This is the perfect riding outfit."

"What's so perfect about it?" George asked.

"First of all, I always wear riding boots because of the mud," Mandy said.

"My shoes are already dirty," Bess said unhappily.

Mud was oozing up around the sides of Nancy's gym shoes, too. But Nancy was too excited to think about it.

"You should wear jeans because they're easy to wash," Mandy went on. "But the most important thing of all is

my special sweatshirt with a horseshoe sewn on it."

"I have a sweatshirt like that," Katie said. "Only mine has a parrot on it."

"A horseshoe is better than a parrot," Mandy said. "Parrots aren't lucky. Horseshoes are."

"Hi, everyone!" Just then Red and Sue came into the ring. They were each leading a line of ponies. And they were each carrying round, black hats that looked like helmets.

Bess opened her eyes wide. "I didn't know ponies were so big!"

"Don't be scared," Nancy said.

"I'm . . . not," Bess said. But she stayed close to her friends as Sue gave everyone a riding hat that fit just right.

"These hats are to be worn at all times when we ride," Sue said. "Just like when you go Rollerblading or bicycle riding.

Then Red explained how to get up on the ponies.

"Wait until an adult is holding the pony's head," Red said. "Then take the reins with your left hand. Put your left foot into the stirrup. Pull yourself up, and swing your right leg over the pony's back."

"It's easy," Mandy whispered to the others.

"Sue and I are going to help each of you mount," Red announced. "Please wait your turn."

Sue started to help Jackie.

Red smiled at Bess. "Ready?"

"I'm not sure," Bess said. "I feel a little scared."

"Don't worry," Red said. "Some of the best riders were nervous when they first began. I think we'll put you on Butterscotch."

"Butterscotch is *my* pony!" Mandy said.

Red smiled at Mandy. "You're the most experienced rider in the class. I was counting on you to ride Rebel. He's a little friskier, but I know you can handle him."

"Okay, Red. If you think I'm such a good rider, then I'll do it," Mandy said.

9

Nancy watched Bess mount Butter-scotch.

"Take the reins in your left hand," Red was saying to Bess. "Good!"

Nancy hardly noticed when Mandy walked over to a glossy black pony.

"What's Mandy doing?" George asked. "She's not supposed to get on the horse by herself."

Nancy turned in time to see Mandy climbing up on Rebel's back. The pony let out a low whinny and pranced sideways.

Nancy saw Mandy try to pull herself up, but she was slipping as Rebel moved! Nancy had to do something fast, or Mandy was going to fall off.

2

Bess's Earrings

Nancy rushed over to Sue. "Mandy needs help!" Nancy called.

Sue looked over and saw Mandy hanging on to Rebel's side. The pony was stomping his feet. His eyes looked wild.

"Whoa, Rebel," Sue called. She hurried over and helped Mandy climb into Rebel's saddle. Once Mandy was seated, the pony calmed down.

"Mandy, what were you doing?" Sue demanded. Nancy thought she sounded angry.

"Getting up on Rebel," Mandy said. Her lower lip was trembling.

"You know the rules about getting on

11

the ponies," Sue said. "Wait for help. You could have hurt yourself."

"Well, I'm sorry!" Mandy said in a huffy voice. "It was no big deal."

Sue helped Nancy mount a chestnut-colored pony named Cupid. George rode Smokey, a black-and-white pony.

Once everyone had mounted, Sue had the horses form a line. Then she led the class around the ring. Red stood by the fence in case anyone needed help.

Nancy felt nervous at first. She wasn't used to being so high off the ground. She was much higher than when she rode her bicycle. But Cupid seemed gentle and walked slowly. Before long Nancy began to relax.

Sue showed the class how to sit up tall and straight in the saddle. Then she led the ponies around the ring in a big circle. She told everyone to hold on with their legs.

Nancy smiled at Bess and George as they passed each other in the circle. Riding was fun, she decided. She was happy that she and Bess and George were signed up for two riding classes every week. She couldn't wait until their next class on Monday.

Friday was the day of the spelling bee. Nancy, Bess, George, and Katie were in their classroom.

"Bess, are you wearing earrings?" Nancy asked her friend.

Bess reached up and touched her earlobes. "Yes," she said. "These are my horseshoe earrings. Mandy said horseshoes are lucky. Well, I'm hoping these will bring me luck in the spelling bee."

"You bought special earrings just for the spelling bee?" George asked.

Bess giggled and shook her head. "I borrowed them from Mom."

"Do you have a good-luck charm for the spelling bee?" Nancy asked Katie.

Katie shook her head. "No. But I still think I'm going to win."

Nancy knew that Katie always got gold stars on her spelling tests. Once Katie had noticed that Mrs. Reynolds

had spelled the word *February* wrong on the board.

The bell rang, and the students took their seats. Mrs. Reynolds took attendance. Nancy had butterflies in her stomach. The spelling bee was about to begin!

"Okay, class," Mrs. Reynolds said. "Please line up across the back of the room."

All the kids jumped out of their seats and hurried to line up. Nancy found a spot between Bess and George. Katie stood on George's other side.

Mrs. Reynolds turned her chair around so that she was facing the line. "When it's your turn, I'll pronounce the word for you. Then you'll say the word, spell it, and then say it again."

Nancy remembered the rules. Mrs. Reynolds's class had already had a few practice spelling bees.

Molly Angelo was first in line.

"Molly, your word is *adopt*," Mrs. Reynolds said.

"Adopt," Molly said. "A-D-O-P-T. Adopt."

"Very good." Mrs. Reynolds smiled at Molly.

The next few students in line got their words right, too. Peter DeSands was next.

"Peter, your word is *banner*," Mrs. Reynolds said.

"Banner," Peter said. "B-A-N-E-R. Banner."

"I'm sorry, Peter," Mrs. Reynolds said. "That's not quite right. You may sit down."

Peter made a face as he walked back to his desk.

Bess was next. "Banner," she said. "B-A-N-N-E-R. Banner."

"That is correct, Bess," Mrs. Reynolds said.

Bess beamed and touched her earrings.

Nancy smiled at Bess. She knew that Bess has gotten the word right because she was a good speller.

Next it was Nancy's turn. Her word

was *gentle*. She got it right. George and Katie got their words right, too.

Phoebe Archer, Jason Hutchings, and Jenny Marsh missed their words. They had to sit down.

"That's the end of round one," Mrs. Reynolds said when everyone had taken one turn. "Now let's start round two."

Mrs. Reynolds gave Molly another word to spell. Then Bess got her second word right.

Nancy felt nervous. She was next!

"Nancy, your word is *beagle*," Mrs. Reynolds said.

One of Nancy's favorite books was called *One Hundred and One Dog Breeds*. Beagles were one of the breeds. Nancy breathed a sigh of relief. "Beagle," she said. "B-E-A-G-L-E. Beagle."

"Very good," Mrs. Reynolds said.

George's word was *familiar*. She left out the second *i*, and had to sit down.

At the end of round two, only five spellers were still standing. They were

17

Brenda Carlton, Bess, Nancy, Katie, and Andrew Leoni.

Bess smiled at Nancy. "I can't believe I haven't made a mistake yet," she said. "These earrings are super-lucky."

"It's not just the earrings," Nancy said. Nancy knew Bess always studied for spelling tests. And she usually got most of the words right.

Round three began.

Brenda made a mistake spelling the word *capitalize*. She stomped back to her seat.

Bess's word was *merry*. She got it right.

Nancy was next. "Your word is *sufficient*," Mrs. Reynolds told Nancy.

Nancy gulped. She thought she had been given a hard word. "Sufficient," Nancy said slowly. "S-U-F-F-I-C . . ." Then she paused. "E-N-T. Sufficient," she said.

"No, I'm sorry," Mrs. Reynolds said.

Nancy felt disappointed as she walked back to her seat. But she wasn't upset. She listened carefully as Katie spelled the word.

"S-U-F-F-I-C-I-E-N-T," Katie said. "Sufficient."

"That is correct," Mrs. Reynolds said.

Nancy realized that she had left out the second letter *i*.

Andrew spelled his next word correctly, too.

Now only Bess, Katie, and Andrew were left standing. Nancy felt happy that Bess was doing so well.

Andrew left out the letter *e* from the word *volume*.

Katie and Bess were the only spellers left!

"Anchovy," Mrs. Reynolds said to Katie.

Katie didn't even stop to think. "That's easy," she said. "Anchovy. A-N-C-H-O-V-I-E. Anchovy. It's spelled just like Katie."

"I'm sorry, Katie, that's not right," Mrs. Reynolds said.

Katie's mouth dropped open. "Are you sure?" she asked Mrs. Reynolds.

"Yes," Mrs. Reynolds said.

Katie stomped back to her desk without saying a word.

Uh-oh, Nancy thought. Katie sure is angry.

The teacher turned to Bess. "Bess, if you can spell the word *anchovy* correctly, you'll be our classroom spelling champ!"

3

Katie's Mad

Nancy took a deep breath. She was nervous just watching Bess spell. She could imagine how nervous Bess felt! Nancy hoped her friend would get the word right.

Bess rubbed one of her horseshoe earrings. "Anchovy," she said. "A-N-C-H-O-V-Y. Anchovy."

"That is exactly right!" Mrs. Reynolds exclaimed. "Bess, you're going to represent our class in the schoolwide bee. Congratulations!"

"Thanks!" Bess said with a smile. She gave George and Nancy the thumbs-up sign.

Katie raised her hand. "Mrs. Reynolds, suppose Bess gets sick," she asked. "Who will be in the spelling bee?"

"Well, you're the runner-up, so you'd represent our class, Katie," Mrs. Reynolds said gently. "But let's all hope that Bess doesn't get sick."

"I'm proud that you won our class's spelling bee," Nancy told Bess at lunch.

"I can't believe you knew how to spell all those words," George added. "You were awesome!"

Bess shook her head. "I never expected to win," she said. "I'm just glad that Mandy told me that horseshoes are lucky. Those earrings must have helped me spell better."

"Shh," George said. "Mandy is sitting right over there. If she hears you, she'll start bragging about how you couldn't have won without her."

Nancy laughed. Mandy had bragged a lot the afternoon before. Mandy wanted everyone to know that her outfit was best and her pony was the most difficult to ride.

Nancy was happy that Mandy had found something she was good at. Mandy had been the worst skater in their ice-skating class.

Katie walked past the girls' table.

"Hey, Katie!" Bess called. "Come sit with us."

"No, thanks," Katie said. She walked right by them. Then she sat at another table.

"I think Katie is mad at me," Bess said.

"She was definitely angry when she lost," Nancy said. "I think she's hoping you'll get sick on the day of the school-wide bee."

"Well, I'm not going to get sick," Bess said. "I want to win."

"Don't worry about Katie," George said. "She'll get over losing in a couple of days."

"Look," Nancy said. "Here comes Mrs. Oshida. I think she's going to make an announcement."

Mrs. Oshida was the assistant principal. She walked by the girls' table and stood in front of the room.

"Attention, please!" Mrs. Oshida called. "I'd like to ask all of the students who won class spelling bees this morning to come to the front of the lunchroom."

Nancy smiled at Bess. "That's you!"

Bess put down the apple she was eating. Then she walked to the front of the cafeteria. She was joined by the other winners.

"Look," Nancy said to George. "Jackie is up there, too."

"Maybe just being around horseshoes was lucky for her," George said.

Nancy shook her head and laughed. She knew George was just joking.

"I want to thank everyone for taking part in the spelling bees this morning," Mrs. Oshida said. "Let's have a round of applause for our winners!"

George and Nancy clapped hard.

Bess was grinning.

Nancy glanced around the lunchroom. Almost everyone was applauding. But Katie had her arms folded across her chest. She was frowning.

Nancy liked Katie. She was sorry that Katie was disappointed about losing the spelling bee. But Nancy didn't think Katie was being a good sport. And she wasn't being fair to Bess.

"The schoolwide bee is next Friday," Mrs. Oshida announced. "That's exactly one week away. Whoever wins will go on to represent our school in a citywide bee. After that there are state competitions and even a national competition in Washington, D.C.

"Now I have some special gifts for today's winners," Mrs. Oshida said. She told the students that each of the winners would get a book called *The Wonderful World of Words*. She called out the names of the winners one at a time. She handed each one a book.

"Bess Marvin will represent Mrs. Reynolds's third-grade class," Mrs. Oshida announced as Bess walked up.

"Hurray!" Nancy and George called.

Bess gave Mrs. Oshida a huge smile as she took her book. Then she hurried back to her seat.

Mrs. Oshida continued to hand out books. "Jackie Taylor will represent Mrs. Costello's fifth-grade class," she said.

Jackie stepped forward. But she didn't look happy. She grabbed her book and ran back to her table.

"What's the matter with Jackie?" Nancy asked.

"I think she might be crying," Bess said. "She was standing near me, and I could hear her sniffling."

"Let's find out," George said.

Nancy, George, and Bess got up and went over to Jackie's table. Jackie's face was wet with tears. Some of her friends were trying to cheer her up.

"Jackie, what's wrong?" George asked.

"She's upset because she won the spelling bee in our class," one of Jackie's friends explained.

"Why?" Nancy was surprised.

"I don't want to be in the schoolwide bee!" Jackie exclaimed.

4

Stage Fright

Why not?" Bess asked. "I think it sounds like fun. We get to stand on the stage. And everyone will be watching us."

"That's the part I hate," Jackie said. "I hate getting up in front of people. I almost threw up during the Thanksgiving play last year!"

Nancy wished she could say something to make Jackie feel better.

"I have an idea," Bess said. "There's something that helped me this morning."

Jackie looked a little more hopeful. "What?" she asked.

"You should get a good-luck charm,"

Bess suggested. "I never would have won without my horseshoe earrings."

Jackie looked thoughtful. "Maybe I'll try that," she said.

Nancy felt like groaning. She didn't believe the horseshoe earrings had helped Bess. And she didn't think a good-luck charm would help Jackie, either.

Mr. Drew took Nancy shopping on Saturday afternoon. She got a book about horses and a pair of boots to wear for riding.

Nancy wore her new boots to the stables on Monday.

Mandy rushed over as soon as Nancy, Bess, and George walked into the stable. "I see you took my advice," Mandy said.

George groaned. "Mandy, you're not the first person to wear boots. Lots of people wear them when they go riding."

"Nancy didn't—not until I told her to," Mandy said.

George and Nancy looked at each other. Mandy's bragging was getting to be too much.

"I took your advice," Bess told Mandy. "I got some horseshoes."

Mandy glanced at Bess's earrings and wrinkled her nose. "You're wearing earrings riding?"

"Not just any earrings," Bess said. "Lucky ones. I wore these during our class spelling bee, and I won! I'm never going to take them off. I want to be lucky every day."

George stared at Bess. "You're never taking them off?"

"Nope!" Bess grinned. "I don't want to fall off Butterscotch."

"Oh, you couldn't fall off Butterscotch," Mandy said. "She's a gentle pony. Not like Rebel."

"Maybe," Bess said. "But I'll feel much safer with my earrings on."

"Red told me he was going to teach you guys how to trot today," Mandy said in her know-it-all voice. "Trotting is very bumpy. Your earrings will probably fall off and get lost in the mud."

"Do you really think so?" Bess asked.

Mandy nodded. "Trust me. I know how to trot."

"Well, okay," Bess said. "I'm going to go put them in my lunch box. Don't let the class start without me."

Bess hurried into the tack room. She got back just as Red and Sue were leading the ponies out.

Nancy thought that the second riding lesson was even more fun than the first. Red showed the class how to get the ponies moving in a trot.

Nancy gently squeezed Cupid's sides with her lower legs. The pony began to move faster. Cupid's back also moved up and down. Nancy felt as if she were riding a wave.

"Once you get the hang of trotting, it will feel just as smooth as walking," Red called.

Nancy looked over at Mandy. She wanted to see how a more experienced rider trotted. But Mandy was bouncing

around in her saddle. She wasn't smiling or laughing. Nancy thought she looked scared.

At the end of the lesson, Red and Sue helped all the riders dismount.

"Now we're going to have a parade," Red announced. "Each one of you can lead your pony back into the stable."

Sue checked to make sure everyone was holding the reins correctly. She reminded the class to stay on the ponies' left sides. Then the parade began. Mandy went first because she had done it before.

Nancy led Cupid into his stall. Then she went into the tack room with Bess and George. George's mother had driven them to the stables that afternoon, so Nancy had to get her school things.

" 'Bye, Nancy," Jackie said as she headed toward the exit.

" 'Bye!" Nancy called.

Katie walked past, too. But she didn't say goodbye to Bess or Nancy or George. Nancy thought Katie was acting silly.

"Oh, no!" Bess yelled. She was staring into her lunch box.

"What's wrong?" Nancy asked.

"My lucky earrings are gone!" Bess cried.

5

Two Suspects

Nancy and George rushed over to Bess.

"Do you think you could have dropped the earrings?" Nancy asked. "You were in a rush to get back out to the ring before the class started."

Bess shook her head. "No. I put them right inside my lunch box, and now they're gone."

"Dad always tells me to retrace my steps when I lose something," Nancy said. "So, let's start with your lunch box."

Bess opened her lunch box wide. All that was inside was Bess's thermos. Nancy peered inside the thermos. All she found were a few drops of milk.

"Maybe the earrings fell out," George said. She got down on her hands and knees and looked under the benches and cubbies.

"Can you see them?" Bess asked.

"No," George said. She got up and brushed off her muddy hands and knees.

"Where was your lunch box?" Nancy asked.

"In that cubby." Bess pointed.

Nancy poked her head into the cubby Bess had used. She ran her hand along all of the cubby walls. She didn't find anything. She checked all the other cubbies. They were empty, too.

"Do you think someone took my earrings?" Bess asked.

"Maybe," Nancy said. She looked carefully on the ground in front of the cubbies. She noticed some of the footprints had squiggly lines in them. The squiggles looked like the letter *S* printed backward.

"If your earrings were stolen, the

thief might have made these footprints," Nancy said.

"Or we could have made them just now," George pointed out.

"We can check," Nancy said. "Let's all make footprints."

Bess, George, and Nancy pushed their shoes into the muddy floor. None of their footprints made squiggly lines.

"So those footprints might belong to the person who stole my earrings," Bess said.

"Maybe," Nancy said. "Lots of people come in and out of the tack room." She took another look at the footprints. She wanted to remember what they looked like.

"We'd better go outside," George said. "I'll bet my mom is waiting."

The girls walked out to the driveway. Mrs. Fayne hadn't arrived yet. They sat on a stone wall to wait.

"Don't worry, Bess," George said. "We'll find your earrings."

"We'd better," Bess said. "Otherwise, I'll never do well in the spelling bee."

"That's not true," Nancy told Bess. "You won the spelling bee because you're a good speller."

"I was a good speller last Friday," Bess said. "But that was only because I had those earrings. I'm going to be a terrible speller in the schoolwide bee. You guys have to help me find them!"

Nancy didn't believe that Bess's earrings were lucky. But Bess believed they were. Maybe someone else did, too.

"If the earrings were stolen, someone in our riding class probably took them," Nancy said. "I wonder who needs good luck."

"Someone who's going to be in the spelling bee," George said.

"Jackie!" Bess exclaimed.

Nancy frowned. "Why would Jackie steal your earrings?"

"Well, she was worried about the spelling bee," Bess said. "Maybe she couldn't find another good-luck charm."

"Maybe . . ." Nancy said.

"Or maybe Katie took the earrings," George said.

Bess and Nancy were quiet for a moment. Katie was their friend. Nancy didn't like the idea that she would do something to hurt Bess.

But Katie hadn't been very nice ever since Bess had won the spelling bee. Maybe Katie was so angry that she took the earrings, Nancy thought.

Mrs. Fayne still hadn't arrived. So Nancy took her special blue notebook out of her book bag. She used the notebook to write down clues when she was solving a mystery. Then she took out a pen.

George and Bess watched as Nancy opened to a fresh page. She wrote "The Case of the Missing Good-Luck Charm" at the top of the page. Under that she wrote one word: "Suspects."

"Put down Jackie's name," Bess said.

"Okay," Nancy said. "Even though I can't believe she's a thief."

"I think you should put down Katie, too," George said.

Nancy wrote down Katie's name.

"Now we have to list the clues," George said.

"How many do we have?" Bess asked.

"Only one," Nancy said. She skipped down a few lines and wrote "Clues." She tapped the pencil eraser against her notebook for a few seconds. Then she wrote "Footprints with squiggly lines."

"Here comes Mom!" George exclaimed as the Fayne family's car pulled into the drive.

Nancy closed her notebook. I'll think more about the case tonight, she told herself.

That evening Mr. Drew came into Nancy's room. "Working on your homework, Pudding Pie?" he asked.

"I already finished," Nancy told him. "Now I'm trying to solve a mystery."

Mr. Drew sat on the edge of Nancy's bed. "I know a little something about mysteries," he said with a smile. "Tell me about it."

Nancy's father was a lawyer, and he often helped Nancy with her cases.

"Bess's earrings are missing," Nancy said. "We think someone may have taken them."

"What makes you think that?" Mr. Drew asked.

"They disappeared in the middle of our riding class," Nancy said. "Whoever took them might have wanted to keep Bess from winning the big spelling bee."

"What does the spelling bee have to do with the earrings?" Mr. Drew asked.

"Bess thinks the earrings are lucky," Nancy said. "She thinks she can't win without them. I tried to tell her that's silly. But she wouldn't listen."

"Well, remember what I always say," Mr. Drew said.

"I know," Nancy said. "Stay cool. Think clearly. And don't jump to conclusions. Don't worry, Daddy. I didn't forget."

"That's my girl," Mr. Drew said as he smoothed Nancy's reddish blond hair.

"Good night, Daddy," Nancy said as Mr. Drew closed the door behind him.

On Tuesday morning Nancy and her friends stopped at their cubbies to put away their lunches, jackets, and books.

"We need more clues," Nancy told Bess and George.

"I have an idea," George said. "Maybe one of the ponies ate Bess's earrings. After all, they were in her lunch box."

"Ha, ha," Bess said sadly. She pulled a piece of paper out of her cubby. "Where did this come from?" she said. She opened the paper and started to read.

"Let's look for clues again during our riding lesson on Thursday," Nancy said.

"I don't think we have to wait until Thursday," Bess said with excitement. She held up the paper. "Listen to this note. It says: 'Drop out now, or you'll be sorry'!"

6

The Faded Clue

Can I see that?" Nancy asked Bess.

Bess handed the note to Nancy.

Nancy looked at the note carefully. She could tell it had been printed out from a computer. She noticed the type was faded on the left side of the page.

" 'Drop out now,' " Nancy read. "I wonder what you're supposed to drop out of."

"School?" George suggested.

"No, silly!" Bess exclaimed. "The spelling bee."

"It must be the spelling bee," Nancy said. "No one would want you to drop out of school."

"I think Katie wrote it," George said.

"She's been acting very unfriendly. And she knows she'll get to be in the spelling bee if Bess drops out."

"I wonder if Katie got a computer recently," Nancy said. "This note was written on a computer."

"She wouldn't need a computer of her own," George said. "Besides, I can tell this note was printed right here at school," she added.

"How can you tell?" Nancy asked.

"The type is all faded down the left side of the page. That's how the printer at the computer lab prints," George said.

Nancy examined the note more carefully. "I think you're right," she said. "I wrote a letter to Aunt Eloise in computer lab last Thursday. When I printed it out, the page was faded just like this."

"But our classroom spelling bee was Friday," Bess said. "We had computer lab on Thursday. How could Katie have written the note telling me to drop out if we had our spelling bee after our computer class?"

"That's true," Nancy said. "And the computer lab is kept locked all the time. No one is allowed in except when we have our classes."

Nancy felt relieved. She hadn't wanted Katie to be guilty. But that meant they still had to find Bess's earrings. And the schoolwide spelling bee was only three days away.

"Let's check out the computer lab after school today," Nancy said. "I want to look at the schedule. Maybe it will give us a clue."

"If there's a clue, we'll find it," George said.

"I hope so," Bess said with a frown. She pulled out *The Wonderful World of Words* from her cubby. "If we don't find my lucky earrings soon, I'm going to have to spend the next three days studying this!"

At the end of school on Tuesday, Nancy, Bess, and George went down to the computer lab.

Carl Sandburg Elementary School's

computer lab was in the basement. It was between the two kindergarten classrooms and across from the art room. Each class visited the lab once a week. The teachers kept a schedule on the door.

The computer lab was locked. But the schedule was taped to the window.

Nancy took out her blue notebook. "I want to write down each class that's been in here since the spelling bee," she said.

George stood on her tiptoes so that she could read the schedule. "Mrs. Keller's class was here on Friday morning," she said. "They were here right before lunch."

"That's one clue," Nancy said. "If someone was in computer lab right before lunch, they wouldn't have known that Bess won our class's spelling bee. Mrs. Oshida didn't announce the winners from all the classes until Friday at lunch."

Nancy made a note in her notebook. "Whoever wrote Bess that note might

have done it in computer lab Friday afternoon or on Monday."

"You're right!" George said. She looked at the schedule again. "Mrs. Beran's class was here on Friday afternoon."

Nancy wrote that down in her notebook. "Are any of our suspects in Mrs. Beran's class?"

Bess thought for a moment. "No," she said. "Mrs. Beran teaches sixth grade. I don't think there were any sixth-graders at the stable yesterday."

"Which classes were here yesterday, on Monday?" Nancy asked George.

"Mrs. Apple's class was here in the morning," George said. "And then Mrs. Costello's class was here in the afternoon."

"Jackie is in Mrs. Costello's class!" Bess said. "She could have written the note and printed it out when her teacher wasn't looking."

Nancy nodded. "It looks as if Jackie is our main suspect. We're going to have to watch her carefully at our riding class on Thursday."

Wednesday was a wet, rainy day. So was Thursday.

"Rain, rain, go away," Bess said when Mrs. Fayne dropped off George, Nancy, and Bess at the stables after school.

"Come again some other day." Nancy finished the nursery rhyme for Bess. "I like the rain, though," she added.

"Me, too," George said. "It makes great puddles!" George was wearing knee-high rain boots. She jumped into a puddle with both feet.

Bess hopped sideways to keep from getting splashed. "Cut it out, George," she said. "You're getting my new riding pants dirty."

"Sorry," George said.

"This weather is part of my bad luck," Bess said as the girls walked toward the stable. "It wasn't raining before my earrings were stolen. We have to find those earrings soon!"

The girls walked into the ring. Katie and Mandy were already waiting. Nancy saw that Mandy was still wearing her special riding outfit. Only now she had added a shiny yellow rain slicker and hat.

Bess nudged Nancy. "Here comes Jackie," she whispered. "Watch for clues."

Nancy nodded.

Jackie came over to talk to them. "Hi," she said in a soft voice.

"Hi," Nancy said. She studied Jackie carefully to see if Jackie looked guilty. But Jackie looked the same as always.

"Have you been studying your spelling words?" Jackie asked Bess. "The spelling bee is tomorrow."

"I know," Bess said. "I'm getting nervous."

"I'm nervous, too," Jackie said. "But I did what you said. I got a good-luck charm."

"What kind of good-luck charm?" Nancy asked.

"A four-leaf clover pin," Jackie said.

"My aunt Alice gave it to me. She bought it in Ireland."

Nancy and Bess looked at each other. They were both thinking the same thing. If Jackie had a good-luck charm of her own, why would she need Bess's earrings?

7

Butterscotch

Hello!" Red called as he came out into the ring. "I'm glad to see that a little mud hasn't scared anyone off. We have a special treat today. We're going on a trail ride."

"Hurray!" Nancy and George yelled.

After everyone had mounted the ponies, Red got onto his horse, Midnight. Then he led the line of ponies out of the ring and into the woods. Sue rode at the back of the line on her horse, Blaze.

Cupid calmly followed Rebel, the pony in front of them on the trail. Nancy liked being up high on Cupid's back. She could reach up and touch the branches of the trees on either side of the trail.

"Isn't this fun?" she called to Mandy.

Mandy didn't answer.

Nancy shrugged. Maybe Mandy didn't hear me, Nancy thought.

After riding for about half an hour, Red led the way out of the woods. Nancy could see the stable and ring just across the field.

"You did a great job, everyone," Red called when they had gotten back to the ring. "Please dismount and lead your ponies back into the stable."

Nancy waited until Sue was watching. Then she took her right foot out of the stirrup. She swung her right leg over Cupid's back, the way Red had taught her.

"Good," Sue said.

Nancy slowly lowered herself to the ground. She took Cupid's reins in her right hand and started toward the stable.

Mandy and Rebel were right in front

of her. Each time Mandy took a step, she sank into the mud.

Nancy hopped from one of Mandy's footprints to the next. Something about those squiggly lines in the mud looks familiar, she thought.

Then Nancy realized what it was. Mandy's boot prints where the same as the ones Nancy had seen in the muddy tack room!

Nancy gently pulled back on Cupid's reins. She waited for Bess and Butterscotch to catch up. George and Smokey were in the back of the group.

"Bess, Mandy's in Mrs. Keller's class, isn't she?" Nancy asked.

"I think so," Bess said. "Why?"

Nancy smiled. "I think I know who took your earrings!"

"Who?" Bess asked with excitement.

Nancy looked around quickly. "I'd better wait to tell you and George when we're inside," she whispered.

Nancy and Bess put their ponies in their stalls. Then they hurried over to George.

"I saw Mandy's footprints," Nancy said in a low voice. "They match the ones we saw in the tack room. I think Mandy is the thief."

George opened her eyes wide. "Let's go talk to her," she said.

Nancy, George, and Bess found Mandy hurrying out of Rebel's stall. Nancy thought that Mandy seemed to be rushing to leave.

"Mandy Trout, we have to talk to you," Bess announced.

"Right now." George put her hands on her hips.

"What do you want?" Mandy asked nervously.

"We want to know why you took Bess's earrings," Nancy said.

Mandy looked at the ground. "How did you know it was me?" she asked softly.

Nancy pointed to Mandy's boots. "Your riding boots gave you away. We saw the prints in the tack room."

"Oh," Mandy said.

"Did you write me that note?" Bess demanded.

"Yes," Mandy said softly. "I wrote it in computer class on Friday morning."

"That's strange," Nancy said. "How did you know Bess was going to win our class's spelling bee? Mrs. Oshida didn't announce the winners until lunchtime."

Mandy looked up. Nancy thought she looked confused. "Spelling bee? Why should I care about the spelling bee? I'm a terrible speller."

"But your note said 'Drop out now, or you'll be sorry,' " George said.

"I wasn't talking about the spelling bee," Mandy explained. "I wanted Bess to drop out of riding lessons."

"Why?" Bess asked.

Mandy's face turned red. She glanced at the big pony in the stall behind her. "I'm scared of Rebel," she whispered. "I want Butterscotch back."

"Why didn't you just tell Red?" Nancy asked.

Mandy sighed. "Because Red thinks

I'm a good rider. I wanted you to think I was a really good rider, too. All of you skate better than I do, even though I'm older. It isn't fair."

"But if you'd told us the truth, we could have talked to Red," Nancy said. "We would have switched with you."

George nodded. "I'd love to ride Rebel," she said. "I think Smokey is a little too slow for me."

"I don't mind giving up Butterscotch if I get to ride Smokey," Bess said. "Any slow pony is fine with me."

"Come on," Nancy suggested. "Let's go talk to Red now."

The four girls went into Red's office together. Mandy explained how she felt about Rebel.

Red agreed to switch the ponies around at the girls' next lesson. "I'm glad you spoke to me," he told Mandy. "The important thing is that you enjoy yourself while you're here."

"Do you think I could have my earrings back now?" Bess asked Mandy as the girls walked out of Red's office.

"Sure," Mandy said. "I've been keeping them safe in my backpack."

Mandy unzipped a tiny pocket inside her backpack. She took out the earrings and handed them to Bess.

"Another mystery solved," Nancy said as Mrs. Marvin's red minivan pulled into the driveway.

"Just in time, too," Bess said. "The spelling bee is tomorrow!"

Nancy was happy that Bess had her earrings back. But she almost wished she hadn't solved the mystery before the spelling bee. She knew that if Bess won now, she'd think it was because of her good-luck charm.

8

Friends Again

On Friday morning Mrs. Reynolds's classroom buzzed with excitment.

"Okay, everyone," Mrs. Reynolds said after she had taken attendance. "Let's line up. It's time to go to the auditorium for the spelling bee."

Nancy, Bess, and George stood together in line. Bess was dressed up for the bee. She was wearing a new dress with a matching headband and matching tights.

"Do you feel nervous?" George asked Bess.

"No," Bess said. She put her hand up to touch her lucky earrings. "Now that

I have my earrings back, I know I'm going to win!"

George and Nancy looked at each other. Bess was going to be competing against fourth-, fifth-, and sixth-graders in the spelling bee.

Bess is going to need more than luck to help her win, Nancy thought. Nancy knew that Bess hadn't studied very much. Bess thought the lucky earrings would help her win.

Mrs. Reynolds led the class into the auditorium. Bess walked up onto the stage with the other spellers. The rest of Mrs. Reynolds's class sat in the audience.

Mrs. Oshida walked up the steps that led to the stage. "Welcome to the Carl Sandburg Elementary School's school-wide spelling bee!" she said into a microphone that was at the center of the stage.

Everyone clapped. Nancy could see Bess standing in the middle of the line. She stood next to Amara Shane, the spelling champion from Mrs. Apple's class. Bess doesn't look nervous, Nancy thought. But most of the other spellers did, especially Jackie Taylor. Jackie held her arms over her stomach, as if she had a stomachache.

Mrs. Oshida told the spellers to step up to the microphone as each person took his or her turn.

Mrs. Oshida started with the sixth-graders and worked her way down the line.

Jackie was the fourth person in line. Nancy could see that she had something shiny pinned to her dress. Nancy guessed it was her four-leaf clover pin.

"Your word is *mayonnaise*," Mrs. Oshida said to Jackie.

Jackie cleared her throat. "Mayonnaise," she whispered. "M-A—."

Jackie stopped at the second letter. Then she put her hands over her mouth and ran behind the curtain. Mrs. Costello hurried down the aisle and followed Jackie.

Students all over the auditorium began to talk and giggle.

"Poor Jackie," George said. "She looked as if she was going to throw up."

Nancy nodded. "It's just like what happened at the Thanksgiving play."

Mrs. Oshida stood in front of the auditorium and clapped her hands. "Let's continue," she said. She went on to the next speller.

Soon it was Bess's turn.

"Your word is *saddle*," Mrs. Oshida said.

"She has a riding word," George whispered to Nancy. "That's a lucky sign."

Nancy looked at George and shook her head. She thought that George sounded as if she was beginning to believe in good-luck charms, too.

"Saddle," Bess said in a loud voice. "S-A-D-D-E-L. Saddle." Then she stopped. "I made a mistake, Mrs. Oshida. Can I try again?"

"I'm sorry," Mrs. Oshida said. "Each speller gets only one try."

Bess stepped down from the stage

and took a seat in the front row. Nancy could see that Bess looked upset.

"Amara?" Mrs. Oshida said. "Will you try the word, please?"

Amara stepped up to the microphone. "Saddle," she said quickly. "S-A-D-D-L-E. Saddle."

"That is correct," Mrs. Oshida said.

"I still can't believe I missed such an easy word," Bess said. The spelling bee was over. Mrs. Reynolds was leading her students back to class. "And it was my first turn, too!"

"Don't be upset," Nancy said. "You did better than George and I did."

"And you didn't throw up, like Jackie," George added.

Bess tried to smile. But she still looked disappointed. "I guess my earrings weren't as lucky as I thought," she said.

Nancy noticed that Bess looked sad all the way through math and science.

Then it was time for art. Mrs. Reynolds led everyone down to the basement. Bess told Ms. Frick, the art teacher, that she didn't feel well. She put her head down on the art table.

"We have to do something to cheer up Bess," George told Nancy.

Nancy nodded. "I have an idea."

George and Nancy spent the entire period working on a project together.

"Time to clean up!" Ms. Frick called.

Nancy and George quickly finished their project. Then they hurried over to Bess.

"We made you something," Nancy said. She put a rolled-up piece of paper in front of Bess.

"What is it?" Bess asked.

"Unroll it and find out," she said.

Bess unrolled the paper. Nancy and George had made a mini-poster. The poster read: "Best Speller in Mrs. Reynolds's Third-Grade Class Award." The writing was in large letters made from silver glitter. At the bottom was "Bess Marvin" in gold glitter.

"Thank you," Bess said. She smiled and looked at the poster again. Nancy

had put her name at the bottom. So had George.

There was a third name, too.

"Katie signed this!" Bess exclaimed.

Nancy nodded. "She's been wanting to say she's sorry. But she didn't know how."

Bess looked around the classroom. She saw Katie standing by the sink.

Bess slowly walked over to Katie. "Thank you for the poster," Bess said shyly.

Katie smiled. "I'm sorry I was such a bad sport. I wanted to be in the spelling bee so much."

"I'll bet you make it next year," Bess said. "And if you do, I'll let you wear my lucky earrings."

"Thanks," Katie said.

"Just make sure you study, too," Bess said. "And concentrate. That's what I forgot to do."

After lunch Mrs. Reynolds gave the class a worksheet. Nancy did hers quickly. Mrs. Reynolds said Nancy could read or write quietly while the rest of the class finished their work.

Nancy got her detective notebook out of her cubby. She wanted to write down her last entry while she remembered exactly what had happened.

When she opened the notebook, a piece of paper fell out. It was a note. Nancy unfolded the piece of paper. She recognized Bess's handwriting.

The note read: "Friends like you are the best good-luck charm of all."

Case closed.

EASY TO READ-
FUN TO SOLVE!

THE
NANCY DREW
N O T E B O O K S®

JOIN NANCY AND HER BEST FRIENDS
AS THEY COLLECT CLUES
AND SOLVE MYSTERIES

IN THE NANCY DREW NOTEBOOKS®
STARTING WITH

#1 THE SLUMBER PARTY SECRET

#2 THE LOST LOCKET

#3 THE SECRET SANTA

#4 BAD DAY FOR BALLET

**Look for a brand-new story every
other month wherever books are sold**

EASY TO READ—FUN TO SOLVE!

**Meet up with suspense and mystery
in The Hardy Boys® are:**

THE CLUES™
BROTHERS

2389